An I Can Read Book®

THE
STRANGE DISAPPEARANCE
OF
ARTHUR CLUCK

by Nathaniel Benchley

pictures by Arnold Lobel

HARPER & ROW, PUBLISHERS

Library of Congress Catalog Card Number: 67-4151
ISBN 0-06-020478-8 (lib. bdg.)

I Can Read Book is a registered trademark of Harper & Row, Publishers, Inc.

For

Victoria Noyes

diseuse extraordinaire

Arthur Cluck

was a very young chicken.

His mother, Mrs. Cluck,

loved him dearly.

She did everything she could

to make him happy.

She even let him ride on her head,

which is unusual for a chicken.

One morning she awoke
and started to get his breakfast,

and found to her horror

that Arthur was gone!

She set up a great outcry.

"Nobody leave this farm!" she said.

"Everyone stay where you are!

My son Arthur is gone!"

First she asked the duck.

"Have you seen my son Arthur?

He has gone somewhere,

and I don't know where!"

"All chickens look alike to me,"

the duck replied.

"I would not know Arthur

from Adam.

But I will tell you one thing—

this happens every spring.

In the spring a lot of baby chicks

get lost. Don't ask me why."

Then she saw the rooster.

"Where is Arthur?" she asked.

"Have you seen him anywhere?"

"I have been busy crowing,"

the rooster replied.

"I cannot watch the children too."

15

But the cow was more helpful.

"I am sorry to hear it," she said.

"In the barn

lives a barn owl named Ralph.

He knows everything.

Perhaps he can help you."

So Mrs. Cluck went to see Ralph.

"My son Arthur has disappeared,"
she said.

"Can you help me find him?
He is small and yellow,
and knows how to ride
on my head."

"I have seen him do that trick,"
Ralph replied.

"I don't do much daytime work,
but tonight I will stand guard
to see what is going on."
"Thank you," said Mrs. Cluck.
"I miss Arthur
more than I can tell you."

So that night

Ralph stayed in the barn and waited.

He waited

and waited

24

and waited

and waited.

And then,

suddenly,

he heard a noise.

It was no louder

than one whisker

being rubbed

against another.

But he knew

where it came from.

And . . .

. . . he dived!

"Aha!" he cried.

"I got you!"

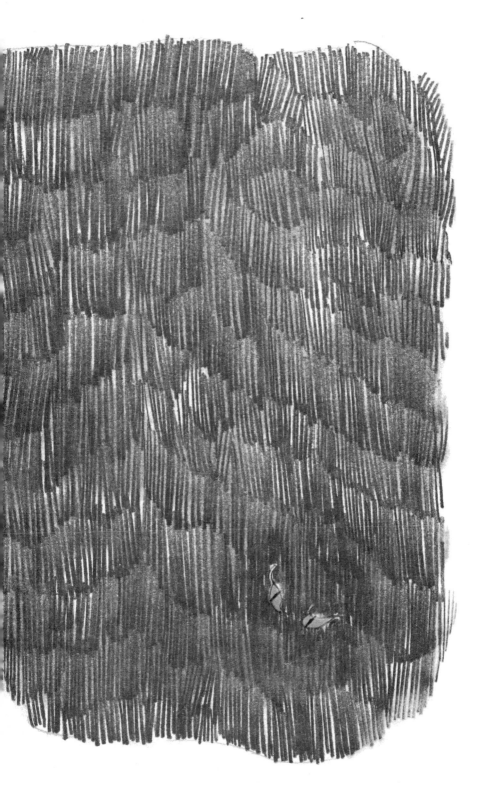

There was a great screech and yowl!

ARRGH! YAP! GRUNCH!

Ralph found that

he was fighting with

a fox!

"Oh, I am sorry!" Ralph said.

"Please excuse me!

I am looking for a baby chicken

named Arthur."

"You chose

a funny way to do it,"

said the fox.

"Do I look

like a baby chicken?"

33

"Now that you mention it, no,"
said Ralph.

"But I thought
you were someone else."

"Thinking is not good enough,"
the fox replied.

"Next time you should be sure."

"I will," said Ralph.

"Believe me,
next time I will be sure."

So back he went on top of his perch.

And the fox went somewhere else.

Then Ralph heard a different sound—

a sound like something being dragged.

He quietly left his perch. Below him,

something was moving on the ground.

It was Gus, the pack rat,

going home

with a heavy load of loot.

"Well!" said Ralph.

"This may lead to what I want."

He followed Gus to where he lived.

Then he leaped

and caught Gus with the loot.

The place was full of things

that Gus had stolen:

rings and string and gum

and marbles and erasers

and glass and teeth and bottle tops

and buttons and a tie clip

and an old tennis ball.

But there was no sign of Arthur.

"Where did you hide

the baby chicken?" Ralph asked.

"Quick, or I might eat you."

"What chicken?" Gus replied.

"I only steal things, not chickens."

Then Ralph saw something interesting

It was an egg

painted in many bright colors.

"Where did you get this?" he asked.

"Up at the farmhouse," Gus said.

"They have a lot of them there."

"That gives me an idea," Ralph said.

"Where there are colored eggs,

there are often baby chickens."

"I have noticed that, too," said Gus.

"But I never thought much about it."

So Ralph flew up to the farmhouse.

It was dark and quiet,

and nobody was about.

51

"This is good," said Ralph.

"It will give me a chance to search."

He looked in the farmhouse window

and saw a bowl of colored eggs.

But he saw no sign of Arthur.

Then he heard something.
In a truck behind the house
he found a crate. The crate
was full of baby chickens.
They were saying,
"Cheep! Cheep! Cheep! Cheep!"

"Arthur!" Ralph called.

"Are you in there?"

"Yes! I am Arthur!"

said one baby chicken.

"So am I!" said another.

"My name is Arthur!" said a third.

"I am Arthur too!" said another.

Arthur had been

a popular name that year.

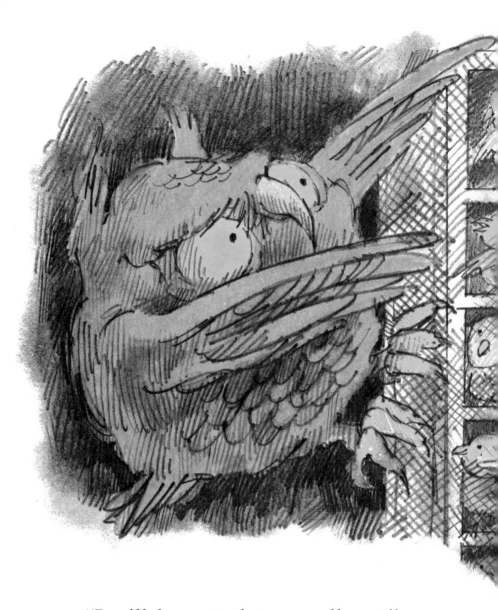

"I will have to let you all out,"

said Ralph. "And the Arthur I want

can come with me."

So he tore at the wire

with his claws.

And pretty soon

the night was full

of baby chickens.

Some went back into the truck,

some went for a walk,

and some fell asleep.

It had been a long day.

61

Of them all, only one Arthur

knew how to ride on someone's head.

It was Arthur Cluck.

And he was more than glad

to go home with Ralph.